Enesee

The History of Dungeon Rock

SALZWASSER
VERLAG

Enesee

The History of Dungeon Rock

Reprint of the original, first published in 1859.

1st Edition 2023 | ISBN: 978-3-37513-680-2

Verlag (Publisher): Salzwasser Verlag GmbH, Zeilweg 44, 60439 Frankfurt, Deutschland
Vertretungsberechtigt (Authorized to represent): E. Roepke, Zeilweg 44, 60439 Frankfurt, Deutschland
Druck (Print): Books on Demand GmbH, In de Tarpen 42, 22848 Norderstedt, Deutschland

THE

HISTORY

OF

DUNGEON ROCK.

COMPLETED SEPT. 17th, 1856.

BY

ENESEE.

SECOND EDITION.

BOSTON:
PUBLISHED BY BELA MARSH,
14 BROMFIELD ST.
1859.

PREFACE.

THE object of the present work is to give a reasonable, and, as far as circumstances will permit, a perfectly true account of the past, present, and future destinies of Dungeon Rock. We do not claim for our book that it is a miraculous production, but simply a natural record of facts, given in a natural way. We assert that the book was dictated by disembodied spirits. And what then? Does it necessarily follow that all spirits are engaged in like work? It may be argued that such thoughts as the history of an earthly place would call up are *low* for spirits. But there is no ground for such a statement, and we refute it in this way:. That there are spirits of every degree, from the lowest to the purest and highest. Of course, somewhere in the rank come in those who are principally, or even wholly, interested in the world. If by that interest they can give to men a truth in lieu of a falsehood, it is so much good done, be it for the lowest den of infamy, for Dungeon Rock, or for the Capitol of the United States, which does, or *ought to*, contain the noblest hearts and the firmest minds which America affords.

At any rate, we ask that our book may be read, and the place
of which it speaks visited, before judgment is passed upon it as
a foolish undertaking, or a senseless work. Spiritualism is
a growing doctrine. It is weaving itself into the every-day
walks of life. We have but one word to say for it, which is,
Investigate. It is all we ask, — all we want.

ENESEE.

HISTORY OF DUNGEON ROCK.

DUNGEON ROCK is as yet only half known. More than "two hundred years ago," when first the foot of civilization pressed the unturned sod of New England's rock-bound soil, a man, past the prime of life, having lost his place in England, determined on seeking a new name in a new country. Accordingly, he embarked with his only earthly treasures, — his wife and the family coat of arms, — and, after a dangerous voyage, reached Plymouth Rock, only to encounter more dangers. And there, in that lonely home, away from all that makes life desirable to childhood, did the little William first see the light of day, and begin the battle of living without love. None but those who have experienced it can tell how deep and terrible is the sternness of a disappointed man.

Ben Wallace — for this was the adventurer's name — had acquired a morbid hate for everything bright and beautiful, and lived, like most of New England's early settlers, for the stern realities of life, expecting nothing but hardships, and, therefore, seeking nothing. No wonder, then, that the aristocratic blood of English ancestry,

1*

coursing through the child's veins, rose against the injustice of being a dependent where he should have been a pride; and, even in his baby days, when the garden was his playground, the unrooted stumps his rocking-horses, and the strips of painted basket material, which he now and then received from the Indian children in the neighborhood, represented to his childish gaze the flags and banners of ancient heraldry, which his mother pointed out to him upon the coat of arms, — even then he defied his father's commands, and turned from his stern reproofs to whisper the childish longings of his own heart to the birds and the dancing stream. " I hate it," he said passionately, when he had arrived at the age of fourteen; " I hate the strong fence that keeps me from finding other people's homes! I hate to be confined to work that I detest, just for the sake of getting food from day to day. I will not do it. The world shall know that William Wallace was not born for no purpose. I will help some one, if it is savages and wild beasts."

Thus spoke the stripling in his lonely home. For six long years did he cherish that one bright thought. It was all the hope he had to stimulate him when labor was his only portion, and life was scarcely worth the danger of preserving it. At last he refused to bear it any longer; and, one pleasant night in the early spring, he dressed himself as near like a native as he could, gathered his own clothes into as small a compass as possible, sprang lightly over the garden fence, and carefully threaded his way through the almost pathless wood to the nearest Indian camp. From there it was an easy task to go further, and he soon began his plans for himself. These were, to get as far from Plymouth as he dared, and still be somewhere in the region of civilization. It was before the foundery was started in Saugus, when only a few stalwart men were discussing the probability of extensive mines in that direction. But Wallace liked the sea-shore; so he built him a residence miles and miles away from any human habitation, determined to assist the first suffering creature that came within his reach. Custom soon came. Little clubs of men often repaired some worn-out canoe, left by the Indians upon the sand, and embarked in it upon the dashing billows to try their luck in procuring fish for food. Almost invariably there would some mishap befall them; and every night the bold young Wallace went to rest with a proud and happy smile curving his delicate lips, and a feeling of true unselfish generosity nestling in his heart. He was happy in his honest calling, and wished for no greater reward than what he received from the natives, and the rough but kind-hearted settlers.

For a short time he lived thus, and his whole soul was in his work. But a change came at last. One fearful stormy night, when the waves rolled far up on the dark sand, and the rain and the wind chanted their wild music, he heard a low moan, instantly followed by a loud cry of agony, and quick calls for help.

He was used to scenes of danger, and, merely supposing that another frail boat had consigned its precious charge to the watery god, and that more human beings were in need of help, he arose, unbarred the low door, and bade the strangers welcome.

Before they entered the house, its inmates — consisting

of a young Scotchman, his fair, pleasant-looking English wife, and their daughter, whose years had been spent in luxury until now, that ten summers had passed above her head, her beauteous home had gone, and she too was destined to a life of labor — were all astir, and the warm fire lighted in the heavy grate.

A tall, well-formed man first entered the room, with a thick frock of shag enveloping his person, confined at the waist by a broad belt, into which was thrust an unsheathed dirk-knife, and a short sword hung suspended by his side. His hat was dripping with water, and his broad shoulders and powerfully built frame made him look, in his unique costume, like a representation of Hercules; while his black hair and eyes, and burlesque manner and motions, gave him the appearance of what he really was, a pirate and a plunderer.

"Give us the most comfortable place in the house," he said, with a careless glance around. "If it had not been for this accursed storm, and the woman aboard, we should not have been obliged to come at all." And he strode out again into the darkness, followed by Jamie Burns, the Scotch emigrant, who was resting there until he could find a home for himself.

"Alice," said the mother, nervously, as she saw the child walk firmly to the open door, "do keep away all you can. If we are all to be murdered, we might as well be cautious about it, as to run into danger with our eyes wide open;" and, turning from the beating rain, she drew the rough oaken chair to the fire, and arranged a fleecy lamb's-wool blanket, which she had brought from home, about its comfortable cushions.

They soon returned. Veale, the first comer, bore a slight girlish form in his arms, enveloped in satin and ermine; her fair pale face forming a strange contrast with the deep crimson hood which fell back from her high white brow, revealing the sunny-hued curls which hung over her rich dress.

There were four other men, in the same dress and having the same general appearance as the first; and, from the noise outside, Wallace concluded there were several more to come.

The men took very little notice of each other, and the lady was beginning to revive under the kindly care of Mrs. Burns, when the voices again approached the door, and, after a short consultation there, three kept on across the beach, and another entered the house.

This last was called Harris by the lady and the men within, who seemed to look up to him as their captain, or, rather, their leader. He appeared the youngest of them all; but there was a lofty look of daring in his dark hazel eyes, and an unfaltering determination in his small mouth, that seemed to quell each motion of familiarity. He looked kindly at the little group huddled around the fire, and gazing so suspiciously at his band of followers. He was rather tall, but very slightly formed, and his dark green frock and crimson sash set off his wild beauty to peculiar advantage.

"Is it far to where you are going, lady?" said Alice, timidly.

The pale face lighted up a moment with pleasure, and, as she turned toward the child, and laid her white dimpled hand on Alice's brown hair, she looked quite like a living being. "I do not know, little one," she answered; "I never was this way before. I wish I did know where we are," she continued, sadly, with a wistful glance at the half-closed door.

"It is only a little way from here," said Harris, soothingly; "see, the moon is coming out already, and we shall soon be on our way." And taking a small compass from his pocket, he adjusted it in the window-frame, as if to shape the course he should take when he left. "Go and unfasten the boat," he said, peremptorily, to one of the men, "and bring up my mantle for your mistress. Quick, man," he added, as the man hesitated; "are you afraid of the moonshine?" and, impatiently opening the rough door, he gazed upon the hurrying clouds and the straggling moonbeams, that half lighted the broken rocks near the dwelling.

The man returned from the water with a large, heavily embroidered mantle, the deep gold-tipped fringe almost sweeping the floor as he threw it over his shoulders to see if it was uninjured. At last they left, just as the gray dawn was breaking. Veale, who seemed to be chief assistant, gave a signal, and the four men marched rapidly down to the water. Harris threw a purse of gold upon the table, and followed Veale, who bore the lady from the house wrapped in the rich mantle.

Wallace looked after them with a dubious, thoughtful look clouding his honest brow. It was long before he heard again from the mysterious visitors, but he kept a more vigilant watch for passing vessels, and answered more readily to unexpected calls than before.

At last they came again. It was night, as before, but

the pale full moon was shedding its pure radiance over the sleeping earth. He was not startled this time. He was alone in the house, and three heavy knocks were heard upon the outer door. They soon entered the house. Four strong, dark-looking men, bearing a huge box, that seemed heavy with something more than its own weight, or the strong irons that bound it, and, as it reached the floor, a dull ring from the inside told a strange tale of darkness. But the men spoke not, except in monosyllables, and Wallace forbore to question them.

As soon as they had found a place for the box they left, and, after being gone some time, returned with another, corresponding in size with the first, but apparently lighter and less firmly secured. As they placed it upon the floor the spring (for there were few locks in those days) flew open, revealing rich dark silks, with heavy gold lace trimmings, small wrought cases of ebony or ivory, and beautiful ornaments of all kinds. They appeared to be not in the least disconcerted, but closed the box again with a loud noise, just as Harris entered with a stranger clad in Spanish citizen's dress. There was a striking contrast in their looks, as Harris raised the elegant bandit cap from his high white brow, and passed his delicate fingers through the short clustering curls, and the stranger flung his heavy slouched hat upon the floor beside him, and stroked his thick, black moustachios with his sun-browned hand.

"We must arrange this matter as quick as practicable," said Harris, in an under tone, apparently continuing their former conversation. "If you have any papers of consequence, I shall expect you to give them up. You can take a small tract of land somewhere near here; or, when we go back to the continent, you can return; but you will be obliged to keep it constantly in your mind that dead men tell no tales, and living ones are not allowed to; — do you understand?" and the youthful leader of that strong band looked fearlessly upon the dark face beside him.

A low mutter of dissatisfaction escaped the swarthy Spaniard as he said, "I want none of your bribes; I want my honest pay."

"Ah! and how much?" said Harris, carelessly.

"Four thousand roubles, which will just pay my forfeiture, and let me back to my own country," was the gloomy reply.

A quick look of intelligent forethought passed over Harris' face, but he only replied, calmly, "You shall have it;" then, turning from the warm fire, he commenced an animated conversation with Wallace concerning his position and its profits.

"Where are your men?" suddenly exclaimed the stranger, rising from his seat, and drawing the heavy folds of his Spanish cloak more closely about his short figure.

"They have gone up the river in the boat, and will soon return," replied Harris.

"Do you reside near here?" asked Wallace.

Harris laughed. "Our traffic is such that it requires us to be constantly on the wing, and we have chosen this as our stopping place," he answered.

Wallace did not notice the reply; he was looking thoughtfully at the heavy chests, and wondering what they contained. Harris saw it; he knew that suspicion was worse than a knowledge; so, carelessly continuing the conversation, he said, "We have a great deal of merchandise to transport, and such cases as these are very useful. This," he said, pushing the spring to one of them, "contains clothing for my wife, Lady Morrillo, which is my native name."

"But these are Spanish goods, I take it," said Wallace, with an earnest look at the nicely-packed box.

"They are," was the reply; "they came from the capital. I had an opportunity to procure them easily; and, besides, I like the Spanish costume for a lady; especially when travelling. See," he continued, raising a delicate jewel-case, and turning the flashing diamonds to the light; "this is of native Spanish workmanship, and there is more beauty than durability to it, I expect."

"Yes," said the stranger, rousing himself from the drowsy sleep into which he had fallen; "yes, that came from the queen's boudoir. I tried hard to save them, but it was no use; the robbers were too strong for us." And with a heavy sigh the man leaned his head against the back of his large chair, and appeared to sleep.

A dark thought flashed across Wallace's mind; but Harris laughed so unconcernedly, and handled the brilliant ornaments with such natural, careless ease, that he forgot his suspicions in their beguiling talk.

"Why do you have the chests made so strong?" Wallace asked after a while.

"O, we need it," he replied, "lifting them in and out the boats; and sometimes we have articles of value to carry. Now, that case has all our most important papers in it. So it is necessary that it should be made strong."

"Yes," said the stranger, again, with more energy than before; "the papers and all that money belong to the Spanish government. It was an infernal mean scheme letting those banditti into the banquet, but little Cristelle was wilful, and fancied their handsome clothes covered honest hearts."

"Come, Don Jose," said Harris, gayly, "do try to wake your sleepy ideas before you talk any more. I presume," he added, turning to Wallace, and noting the dark foreboding that again crossed his brow, "that he refers to some valuable pieces of plate in our possession. You remember when the last rebellion took place the capital was said to have been robbed. At that time the insurgents placed some of their spoils in trust in our hands, and we still retain them. Don Jose is confused to-night; what with the sea-sickness, and the change from cold to warm air, he is nearly insensible;" and he laughed a careless, merry laugh, at the same time casting a look of stern, contemptuous reproof upon the cowering Spaniard.

At this stage of affairs the sound of heavy voices, and the tramp of measured steps, told that the men had returned. Don Jose sprung from his seat with a quick, nervous motion, drew his hat over his dark flashing eyes, and waited impatiently for further motions. Wallace opened the door, and, as he supposed, the same four men that brought the boxes entered to remove them. He was deceived, however, by their dress; the whole band, consisting of between thirty and forty members, dressing alike, excepting the five leaders and Harris, who, although he had not yet reached the twenty-second year of his age, was universally acknowledged as leader of the whole; his father having held that place until his death, which occurred two years before.

And now the tangled thread of our history leads us back, three long and changing years, to a small thatched cottage in Italy, where all day long the air is heavy with perfume, and the sun goes down at eventide in a sea of purple, and crimson, and gold.

"Mother, you do wrong to judge Morrillo so harshly," said a low, sweet voice, one midsummer night. "True he wears the bandit frock and cap, but I know they hide a noble head, and shield a generous heart. Besides he is so young now, that his father's will is the only law he knows; he never had a mother to tell him how to live." And the voice was low and sad, and the slight form of Arabel Ortono glided away from the drooping vine she was trailing, and sought her favorite retreat in the shaded veranda.

Her mother soon sought her there, and paused a moment in the low, arched doorway, to contemplate the picture before her. Arabel was kneeling in a shaded niche, her fair young face flushing and paling alternately, her long golden-brown curls sweeping over the closely-fitting spencer of darkest hue, and her eyes raised to catch the brightest moonbeams as they struggled through the thick vines.

"Well, Arabel," said the mother, at last interrupting the girl's revery, "you have argued the young pirate's cause pretty faithfully; now let me hear you protect your own. Tell me how, and why, you first became interested

in those most lawless of all unlawful men, and I will try
to be reasonable with your wild fancies."

Proudly the young Venetian rose from her lowly place
and stood beside her mother. "Almost," said the mother,
playfully measuring the girl's height with her eye, "almost as tall as I."

"Yes, mother," answered the girl, "I am at least
large enough to know how to talk reasonably." And a
light, scornful smile flitted over the fair, pale face.

The mother noticed it, but only answering, calmly, "I
am ready, now," she seated herself upon the long, rustic
bench, and prepared to listen.

"Fourteen years ago to-day," Arabel commenced, in
a low, hurried voice, "my father died, and left you with
three small children, myself the youngest, and for that
reason most fondly cherished. 'You must teach them
how to live, Clarette,' I heard him say, one bright, moonlit evening, when you was weeping by his bedside in our
palace home, and we were nestled on the low divan in the
deep windows, trembling and terrified. I remember
every incident of the dark and dreadful days that followed
as well as though it were but yesterday. The heavy
pall with its silver trimmings, the jet-black horses, and
the dark and solemn hearse. Then our house was barricaded; and even you, mother, will not dare to say that
the noble band of Morrillo's followers did not help us
more than all the Venetian police. I saw them then on
that fearful day, and I honored the bandit badge which
bound them to each other. It is to them we owe all we
have here to remind us of our former home; and even if
they have in their possession the most valuable of our

family treasures, it is better so than that our enemies
should have them, is it not?" and the girl paused and
looked calmly into her mother's eyes.

"Yes, Arabel," was the half-stifled reply. "It is
time that you should know what I never dared tell you
before, even though it fixes you more firmly in the purpose I am trying to change. It is to the gray-haired
Morrillo that we owe our present home. All you have
ever known of your father is only what your own childish heart taught you to remember. But there is more
for you to know, and you must know it. Signor Ortono
was a friend to the Venetian emperor at the time when
his enemies were most numerous. When our house was
barricaded, at the time you remember, was when the
opposing party made their grand attack, and impoverished
all the families that did not lend them aid. Ours of course
must have yielded an easy prey, had it not been for the
kindly interference of the pirate robbers, who, though
they took a great deal that rightfully belonged to us, left
us enough to procure a home and live comfortably. And
this was fourtern years ago, when you had reached the
third year of your sunny life. Ever since then I have
heard from them occasionally, and, now—O, bitter fate!
—that my youngest, and, as it were, my only child, should
so forget the high estate of her birth as to look with favor
on the robber's child!" And the mother ceased speaking, but the scornful tones of her voice still rung in the
girl's ears.

"But you have not heard half my story yet," she
said softly, crushing back her rebellious thoughts. "Ten
years ago, when first my sisters went away from their

2*

own home to the vineyard in Orton village, one of the
same band that helped us in our trouble gave uncle Fay
a silver salver with our family crest upon it, because Luella had not turned from her purpose when she was trying to reinstate herself in the family name. And, last
of all, just one short year ago, Morrillo came here in a
pelting storm, and claimed a home for a few hours. We
knew him well, but he had entirely forgotten us. He
feigned no surprise, however, when you recalled those
distant, painful days, but restored with seeming pleasure
all these mementos of the city home. You know, if we
had the most costly articles here, they would be immediately taken from us. He gave us even more than we can
keep in safety, and for all these kindnesses I am very
grateful." And a slight blush deepened on the girl's
cheek as she ceased speaking.

"So it is only gratitude, eh! that calls my Bel so
often down to the sparkling waters of the gulf in the
moonlight?" said the mother, with the same unreconciled
sadness in her voice.

"I care not that you should know it, mother," was
the reply. "I have never yet tried to hide anything
from you. I am proud to acknowledge the acquaintance
of one so noble as Claud Morrillo. It is to meet him
that I wander down the beach when I know the boats are
coming in." And, with a look of forced carelessness, the
young Italian kissed her mother a good-night, and went
to rest with a heavy weight on her proud heart, where a
happy hope had late found birth.

Years pass very rapidly when every day brings its own
task and leaves no time for idleness; and now, almost

before we are aware of it, the luscious autumn is gone, winter withdraws his fleecy mantle, and the spring is growing old. Again the cottage home is hushed and still, the blinds are closed, and no sign or sound of life comes from the silent interior. The gray morning sky is tinted with gorgeous clouds, that gradually deepen toward the east, where they are bursting into one steady glow of crimson beauty. In the little room, that has so long been Arabel's, the same slight form is resting, and the same low voice breathed out the last night's prayer. But a change has passed over her still life, — a change that is felt, but only half realized.

"Dead, dead!" she moaned faintly in her uneasy slumbers; and in the hall below two forms are faintly discernible in the darkened gloom. They are the two older sisters, Christabel and Luella, who have returned from the vineyard to watch over their mother's sickness, and attend to the last sad rites of her burial, — for she was indeed dead, dead.

"It is very hard to have death steal so dear a mother; is it not, Lu?" said Arabel, with childish trust, for grief had made her alike powerless to think or act.

"No, not hard," was the calm reply, "for it was our Father's will. Mother was not used to such a life. It would be selfish in you to wish her back again. You can go to the vineyard with us to-morrow, and then you will soon learn to be your own mother;" and Luella turned away.

"O, not to-morrow!" sobbed Arabel, convulsively. "You will not go to-morrow, Christa?" and she looked tearfully upon her other sister.

"Well, and if you stay another day, will you be any more willing to go?" said the straightforward Christabel.

Arabel pressed both hands upon her brow, as though she would concentrate her scattered thoughts, and said, mournfully, "If you will let me stay until Friday night, I will go anywhere."

"Have you no reason for wishing to remain except your own fancy?" asked Luella, gently.

"I don't know," was the sad reply; "it may be fancy, but I do want to stay."

"Very well, then," said Christa, "we will do as you say;" and so the matter was settled.

Friday night came at last. The furniture was all packed or disposed of. It was arranged that they should leave early next morning, and Arabel wandered out alone to take, as she said, a last farewell of the pleasant gulf of Venice, but in reality to meet Claud again, and tell him her grief, and the new home to which she was going. A long, graceful boat came bounding over the water, and the pale, blue light in the stern distinguished it from every other sailer. Soon its keel ran far up on the sand, and a tall, handsome form sprang out, and, giving a few orders to the rowers, told them when to return for him, then walked on, leaving them to put back. Three times did he and Arabel meet and pass each other, and every time a look of recognition passed between them; but there were laws to govern all their actions, which they both knew, to prevent deception. Then, the hours passed all too quickly for their busy tongues; for there had been many changes since they met before.

"We will not talk so mournfully, any more, Bel. You have been more favored than I, for you have had a mother to love you," said the youth, pleasantly.

"And you than I, for you have had a father to direct," was the sad reply. For it was Claud's task now to comfort the petted child.

The next day the sisters sold the cottage and left for Orton Village vineyard. "I know not how we shall like each other," Luella said; and as an instance of the dissimilarities in their characters, we have but to look at the way they speak of their mother's death.

"She is dead, Claud; my own dear mother is dead," Arabel said, convulsively, stifling her sobs. "O, I can't be proud now, for she is dead!" And, resting her head on his shoulder, she wept her grief away.

Christabel comes next. She was writing to a friend of hers, a vintner whose place joined Ortonville. "My mother is not living," she wrote, calmly, "and, for the future, my home will be just where I chance to stay."

"Just two short nights ago," so spoke Luella's diary, "our only surviving parent went home to the Father who gave her life; her pale hands clasping the silver crucifix to her still heart, and her last faint breath used to speak to her dearest earthly treasures. 'You must be Arabel's mother, Luella, and perform your own life-task well,' was her only counsel to me. To Christa she said still less, doubtless knowing that she had her father's strong intellect and thorough knowledge of human nature. Arabel was her principal thought, and no wonder, either, she is so young and inexperienced. I wish I could remember half that I have heard her say. I won-

der why she said so many times, 'If you would escape
a life of unhappiness, remember what I say, and never,
never wed an infidel.' "

But we are making a short story too long. Suffice it
to say that the girls soon learned to take each her own
place at the vineyard, and direct the laborers at their
work with quiet ease.

"It is not often that we meet now, Claud says," murmured Arabel, after being six months in the vineyard;
"but I know he likes his wild home better than this,
and surely I do, it is so very pleasant to have no con-
finement to certain hours of labor. To-night I am going
again to the fortress—joy! joy!" And she went fearlessly as the wild bird to its mountain nest, trustingly as
the lamb to the shepherd's fold.

Claud was walking on the battlements, with his eyes
fixed upon the ground. Arabel ascended the steps and
commenced the promenade. Four times they met and
passed each other; then, trembling with a strange appre-
hension, she approached and laid her white hand on his
arm. He started as though just awakened from a dream.

"Is it you, Bel?" he said, and pressed a kiss on her
pallid brow, then led her out from the deep shadow to
where they could see the moonlight resting on the waves.

"Claud, I am afraid of you," Arabel said, soberly.
"What makes your hand tremble, and your cheek so
pale?" and she looked earnestly into his face.

"Poor child!" said Claud, sadly. Arabel heard it,
and answered quickly,

"O, Claud, I am not a child! I can bear to know

anything. See how strong I am!" and she drew her
hand from his arm and stood before him.

Claud smiled sadly, and said, "We are twins in sorrow
now; both alone, Bel!"

Slowly the blood left her face, and her hands clasped
nervously together. "Tell me what you mean, Claud,"
she said, as she only half understood him; "tell me if
you have no father!"

"It is even so," was the reply. "My father died since
noon to-day, and now his form is resting in the hall, where
the soft light is gleaming out. Come, we will go and see
how calm he looks in his majestic repose;" and, without
waiting for a reply, he drew her in through the heavily-
wrought curtains to the large, dimly-illumined apartment,
where rested a metal burial-case which contained all that
was earthly of the gray-haired chief, known as Morrillo,
the bandit's pride, there in the gloomy fortress, and as
Claudius Etheredge in the brilliant Roman home. But
none who met him at the brave display of chivalry, or in
the more courtly halls of etiquette, dreamed their haughty
yet affable host was the famous Morrillo, whom they
feared and dreaded.

"He was my own dear friend," Arabel said, in a low
voice. "How will you bury him?" she added, quickly,
thinking of her own parents.

A mournful smile lighted Claud's beautiful face for a
moment as he replied, "To-night the carriage will come
from Etheredge Hall, and to-morrow he will be buried in
state from our royal home. I shall be chief mourner, —
sole mourner, as to that part, — except a few fawning
relatives, who know nothing of the dead except that he is

reputed to leave a princely fortune ; " and a darkly bitter smile crossed the young Italian's face. " I hate such detestable hypocrisy," he said ; " but my father always had it to bear, and I must take his place in everything. So help me, father ! " and he bowed his head, and laid his hand on the cold, damp brow.

Arabel was startled, alarmed, terrified, at his strange words. " How can *he* go to Etheredge Hall ? " she said " Lord Etheredge is away, and does not expect to return for thirty days, at least."

" How know you ? " exclaimed Claud, earnestly.

" By uncle Fay Ortono, who married Lady Emelie Etheredge, half sister to the noble lord," was the reply.

" Then they are not your relatives," he said. " But, tell me, Bel, if you can keep a secret."

She nodded silently and wonderingly.

" What is my name ? " he asked.

" Claud Morrillo," said Arabel, proudly.

Claud smiled sadly, and said, " Yes, to you I am ; but I have two names. Now, mind what I say, Arabel," he said, sternly grasping her arm ; " my father and Lord Etheredge are one and the same person ; and I am now to take his title, and be Lord Etheredge in his stead. But, by the acquaintance we have had with each other, Arabel Ortono, and by the remembrance of our many meetings here, I warn you to tell no one of what I have said to-night."

Then tearfully they parted, that warm, soft night ; Arabel to weep until slumber closed her weary lids, and brought gay visions of future happiness ; Claud to return to the fortress, arrange his father's business, snatch a single hour of deep, unrefreshing repose, and, as the bell on the high tower rung out the mystic midnight hour of twelve, to see his father's form placed in his own private carriage and whirl rapidly away, drawn by his own splendidly caparisoned horses.

As morning dawned, Claud left the fortress in the care of the banditti, and went in a disguised conveyance to his home in Rome, and spent half the hours of that long day in pacing up and down the gorgeous rooms. Friends called, but he steadily refused himself to them; relatives arrived, but he kept from them in scorn. At last another guest was announced. It was Fay Ortono, Lady Emelie and Luella having accompanied him to the burial. Deeply and truly did they sympathize with the young lord, and he appreciated their disinterestedness; for were they not Arabel's nearest friends; and might he not, through them, become better acquainted with her?

At sunset, that night, Lord Etheredge was buried. Waxen tapers were lit in the damp tomb, and heavy, mellow-toned bells tolled out the last requiem of departed worth.

"He is not an infidel!" murmured Arabel, joyfully. "Mother in heaven! Claud is good; for he believes, and the monks have said mass for him!"

Another half-year went by with magic rapidity. Again came the luscious harvest-time, and again the girls were needed more than ever at the vineyard, when death came again; and this time, O terror! uncle Fay was called. The girls worked nobly, so said Lady Emelie; they should be rewarded for it, and so they were; but when winter came, they could stay no longer, and, by

Claud's invitation, they went together to the fortress, and determined to make it, for a short time, their home. There was but one female there at the time, and she was the most silent of her famously loquacious sex. The girls lived very pleasantly together, sometimes for whole weeks seeing no one beside themselves, and again having company every day when Claud was about. But all this time Luella was fading. Her breath came quick and painful, her pale cheeks wore a bright flush, and her firm step faltered. Claud was first to make the sad discovery. He had been away on a cruise, and, upon his return, had taken the fortress for his home once more.

"You shall have all the physicians in Venice," said the silent housekeeper, as she saw how sick the girl was growing, "and the best nurse in all Italy, rather than die so young."

But it all availed nothing; she was dying. Aunt Emelie rode over in her own beautiful carriage to take her back to the vineyard; but she did not go. All the long winter she looked from the high arched windows, and when the warm spring air stole in through the rich, soft curtains, the light reburned in her eyes, and she felt her strength returning. Then they thought she would soon be well, and even she herself was for a short time deceived.

But another subject was now uppermost in their minds. Christa was to leave them for the vintner's home. She was married in the dim old cathedral, and a long train of attendants swept gayly out, for it was grand to be married beneath the roof-tree of the young Lord Etheredge, no one but Arabel knowing that the fortress was the bandit's hiding-place, and she, like a discreet girl, kept her own counsel, and allowed them all to live in blissful ignorance.

Then Arabel was wedded, too, with lilies in her jewelled bouquet-holder, and knots of pearls in her long golden brown curls ; with a long embroidered veil floating round her slight form, and her heavy blonde sleeves caught up with pearls upon the shoulders of her satin spencer. Luella kissed her tenderly as a mother would a happy child, then passed her hands over her smooth, dancing curls, and smiled to see them roll up again.

"I know I look pretty, Lu," Arabel said ; "for when we stood together by the statues, just now, Claud said Luella was a perfect representation of pride perfectly subdued; but Bel was a Diana when moving, and a Madonna when still."

Luella only smiled at her sister's words. She knew Arabel was not vain, and she had no fears for the future when her easy-chair was placed in the large cathedral to witness the brilliant bridal. "Have I no sister now?" she asked, half sadly, half playfully, as Arabel danced by her, all radiant in her glorious beauty.

"Certainly," answered a manly voice beside her ; "she does not love the old friend less, but loves the new one more."

Luella turned quickly, and met a pair of searching blue eyes fixed upon her beautiful face. "I beg pardon, lady," said the man, in a slightly confused tone, "I thought I was a stranger here, but I believe we have met before."

"It may be," said Luella, thoughtfully; "your voice

is familiar, but your looks I have forgotten. Then suddenly remembering herself, she added, "Were you ever
at Orton village vineyard?"

The puzzled look left his face as he replied, "So we
are not entirely unacquainted. May I ask how you
succeeded in the work you was engaged in when we last
met?"

"Very well," was her reply; "even better than I
expected."

"Then you are Lady Ortono?" he persisted.

"Yes; that is, I am recorded so. But I choose to be
called by my own simple name. I am only unwilling to
believe that might makes right."

"You do not mean to say it was from entirely dis-
interested motives that you strove so hard for the name
of Ortono?" said the stranger, wonderingly. "You
had the property restored, had you not?"

"No, Mons. Jerold," she replied; "I have no wealth,
no honor, no family. I honor you and your band for
your steady attachment to each other. I could wish
that the business you follow was more lawful, and the
firmness you evince was in a better cause. Adieu, Mons.
Jerold;" and, with a pleasant smile, and a graceful wave
of her thin white hand, she glided away, leaving the
bandit captain laughing at his own inquisitiveness, and
vexed that he could not be an equal with the fair girl,
who had only her own native pride to support the high
position she had taken.

All those long, warm days, Luella had been lingering
like a spirit, only half confined to earth; and now the
hectic flush burned deeper, and her eyes flashed with re-

newed brilliancy; the blue veins, like a net-work of azure
threads, were traced on her pure brow, and her hands
grew more transparent every day.

With the best medical attendance, and the kindest care
that could be procured, she felt that she was soon to pass
away, and she often spoke of death.

"Bury me down by the water's edge," she said, one
night, when they were watching, from the high windows,
the moonlight on the dancing waves. "Not in the
sparkling sand here by the friendly tower; but away
out, where the shadows are long and dark, where the
pure white cliff is rising in the still night, a watcher
over the gulf. Then, when night comes again, I will
come back to earth and tell you how to live."

And, before another moon had waxed and waned, Luella slept the sleep that knows no waking. And they
buried her under the pure chalky cliff, where she had so
often watched the sea-gulls at the approach of a storm.

Arabel and Christa mourned for their sister, but Claud
had just become interested in the ideas of America as a
grand resort. Arabel was all on the *qui vive* to go; and,
without one regret, with only a parting farewell for
Christa, and an earnest, gentle look at Luella's grave,
she entered the boat with a light step and a light heart,
and bade adieu to her native land perhaps forever. When
they were far out at sea, the last object on which her
eyes rested was the pure white cliff under which Luella
slept. When they came in sight of land again it was only
a single hour past midnight, but the long, loud cry that
rung out from the stationed watch awakened every sleeper,

3*

and called up the eager and curious to catch the first glimpse of land.

"Where are we now?" Arabel said, as she went upon deck, and felt the land breeze sweeping around her, and filling the long, flapping sails.

"We have reached our destination," answered Harris, as Claud directed the sailors to call him, for he felt that it was necessary to have a new name for every place, to prevent suspicion.

Then fourteen of the crew manned a boat, and went ashore to make discoveries; they returned at nightfall, having discovered the place in Saugus known to this day as Pirates' Glen, and still bearing the evidence of having been inhabited. The next day there were heavy black clouds in the horizon, and at night they burst in all their mad fury, causing the black waves to seethe and boil against the rough rocks in sight, and frightening Arabel almost away from her senses.

"We shall die, Claud, I know we shall," she moaned, wearily grasping the silken covering to the lounge on which she lay. Then she fainted. Harris remembered a small public house he had seen upon the beach, and determined that, be the consequences what they might, he would reach that. The men readily volunteered to accompany them, and this brings us back to the point where we started, the night that first gave Wallace an acquaintance with the band of men that afterward frequented *Pirates' Glen*, and *Dungeon Rock*. It was, perhaps, a week that they spent there, and then returned again to Italy; not, however, until they had aroused the suspicions of the settlers, who were on the constant look-out for danger.

A few weeks after their return a great rebellion arose in Spain. Claud must go; Arabel dared not, — so she remained at the fortress, with her own thoughts and the gorgeous works of art for company, and he started on the wild and perilous adventure. When he returned the boats were loaded with costly articles that had the indelible Spanish stamp upon them. These he secreted in the ancient fort. Some were carried away up to their hiding-place in Wales, and others were retained in Spain. The greater part, however, were brought there, and to Arabel's eager, childish questions of where he found them, and what they were for, he only answered, with a sober smile, "They are all to be changed into money, Bel, unless you want some of them to wear."

But he heard flying rumors that he was suspected even there. "That must not be," he said, firmly; "for I dread the idea of being known as a pirate. I cannot, will not, bear it."

So he packed the goods he had stolen from the imperial Spanish palace, all the beautiful adornings of the fair young queen, — for it was she whom Don Jose had called little Cristelle in the first part of our story, — and hid them in the low vaulted basement. Don Jose had been the queen's valet, and Claud took him to be of future use to them in discovering the secrets concerning their enterprise in Spain. Then he opened the doors of the ancient tower and fortress; lighted up the long cathedral, with its dim arches, and quaint oaken carving, and gave his friends in Rome and Venice a banquet, at which he and his young bride presided. The rooms were crowded with beauty and fashion; music floated through the long cor-

ridors, and up and down the winding stairs, covered for
the occasion with rich, soft carpets. The night passed in
revelry, and when morning dawned the guests departed
satisfied.

To Arabel it seemed like a fairy dream of beauty, so
much life and joy around; to Claud it was the hollow
formalities of hypocrisy. He saw the eager glances, the
suspicious looks, the cautious steps, when they entered
the dim old rooms. He could bear his double part well,
however, and he did. It was not long after this that he
carried the most suspicious goods across the water, and
landed them in the then unbroken solitude of Pirates'
Glen.

By this time the foundery was nearly built. All the
men of the place met there to talk over their affairs, and
here it was that Claud, or rather Harris, used to station a
watch, and sometimes he would stay himself to hear what
was said, and direct his own work accordingly.

Arabel had been staying at the Glen several days, and
begged that she might stop still longer,— the woody glade
was so wild, and the distant hills so high. She was not
obliged to practise constant deception there; she would
remain a little while; and she did one whole long day
alone, but she was used to solitude.

That night the band was organized; it was to consist
of six men, with Veale for a leader, making seven beside
Harris. There was another such band in Italy; one in
Spain, the beautiful land of legends and romance; one in
sunny, pleasant France; and one away in muddy Wales,
where meadows are greener and brighter for the stagnant

r beneath, and the ruinous old castle home of a former feudal lord was damp and gray with age.

Two days Arabel remained in the glen alone, then Harris came back from the boat with Don Jose; he appeared almost savage to Arabel, but he soon learned that she was the leader's bride, and could do as she chose.

At this time the first history, that is considered as really authentic, is commenced. A vessel, afterward known as the phantom ship, was seen in the waters off Nahant at or near sunrise. It presented to the eye a strange optical delusion of a ship resting motionless upon the water, and another, the exact counterpart of the first, suspended keel upwards in the air; the masts and rigging of the two apparently touching each other. It was the pirate ship Arabel, that had come too far in at high tide, and was therefore obliged to wait until the water rose again in order to get out to sea.

Don Jose returned to Spain, but his honor was gone, his queen dethroned, and he himself treated like a traitor on all sides. "I'll not have the name without the game, I reckon," he said, with true Spanish bitterness; and, taking his only living relative, a boy about twelve years of age, left him by his sister, he joined the banditti as a wanderer, and not as a resident, determined to wreak his vengeance on the Spanish government.

The next time the pirates came to America, Don Jose and the boy both accompanied them. They landed early in the morning, and the boy Carl took his place in the village as spy. All the long day he wandered up and down, his quick ear catching every suspicious word, and at night, while returning to the place fixed upon as the look-out, he arranged the whole matter in his mind, making an accurate calculation of how many reliable men the settlement numbered when they would make their exploration, etc. By the time he had settled it all in his own thoughts he arrived at "Look-out Hill," or "High Rock," as it is now called. With a light, eager step, he clambered up the rocks, and reached the firm platform upon the top. Soon he espied a moving speck far out upon the blue waves, and immediately hoisting the signal agreed upon, he raised a small glass to his eye, and commenced scanning the distant object. He was dressed in the Spanish costume of that day; but there was as an oriental richness about it which is now lost to the world. It looked more like the Turkish apparel of the present time; the flowing trousers and tunic giving a graceful air to his slender form, and quick, agile motions; and the whole occurrence gave rise to the interesting novelette entitled, "The Child of the Sea."

"What success, Carl?" asked Don Jose, as he came up the long path from the boat-landing, and clasped the boy in his arms.

"The best, father," was the reply, "but they are to have a meeting to-night, which it will be best for some one of us to attend." He then told what he had heard through the day, and with his help the father rehearsed it again to the band.

"I must go," said Harris, springing up and preparing to leave.

"Why you, Sir Harris?" asked several voices.

"For this reason," answered Harris, thoughtfully; "Don Jose has just shown himself incapable of remembering, by being unable to repeat, Carl's story; Veale always needs to hear a story twice, in order to comprehend it; and the rest are not interested enough to understand correctly, or report accurately; therefore I must go, or little Carl," he added, turning to the boy, who rose from his reclining posture and stood beside his commander.

"I am not afraid, signor," he said, firmly; "but it needs an older head and truer skill than mine to study the craft of Englishmen."

"Truly spoken, Carl," answered Harris; "but you shall take my place here," and, pushing aside the heavy sail, he entered a little room arranged for Arabel's accommodation, followed by Carl.

"I am going over to the settlement, Bel," he said, "and have brought you a new valet to entertain you while I am gone; if you like his appearance, he shall be your page for the future."

Arabel raised her eyes from the delicate chess-board, on which she was listlessly arranging the men, and met Carl's earnest, childish gaze, with a pleasant smile. "But, why must you go, Harris? there are enough beside you," she said, turning to him.

"We are liable to be routed from here at any time," he replied, "and I alone can manage the part of spy, and decide when to remove." And away he went, leaving Carl established in his new honors.

"I wish that I might die," said Arabel, passionately, that night, after she had heard Carl's story of the great robbery, and listened to his witching recital of the time when the young queen called him her little page, and he supported her train in passing through the corridor, or held her fan in the audience chamber. He did not know how intimately connected his beautiful mistress and brave young commander were with the robber Morrillo and his powerful band. "I wish I had died long ago in the little cottage by the water-side; not when my mother did; so pure and calm as was her spirit, mine would have looked dark beside it; but, I was wild and thoughtless then. Methinks I have lived a thousand years since that strange brightness passed away. Where are you, mother? O, come back to me, — to your own Arabel!"

Even then there was a raging fever heat in her veins, and a delirious, wildering look in her dark eyes. Long before the morning dawned Harris returned to the Glen. The men noted his mischievous, glancing smile, more than his stern, commanding look, as he came out from the thick underbrush, and waved his hand as a signal for them to stop.

"Have you removed and secured all our valuables?" he asked, "for I have an inkling, from what has been said to-night, that they will soon be on our track."

"We have moved them all," was the reply, "and are now waiting for you to tell us what shall be done with our Madonna to-night. We might leave her there, if we were sure Sir Wolf would wed her before daybreak; but, then, she is a woman, and will be certain sure to do as she is not wanted to."

"Hold your peace, Don Jose!" thundered Harris, "or we will know the reason. I would have you to know that my *wife* is your *queen;*" and there was a slight, mocking emphasis on the words, which brought

and laughing at those who tried to discover the pirates'
treasures, was told, beside the fire, in the long winter
evenings, until at last it was thrown aside as a superstitious falsehood, and · now is only remembered in a few
families as a quaint legend of former years.

. It was only two short days from then that Harris returned, but Bel was a spirit. The excitement of those
fearful hours had been too much for her. She drew the
downy, silken couch to the side of the spring in the
rock, where the clear water fell from the crevices above,
with a musical tinkle, into a large open basin below, and
there, in that silent room,

> " She rested her fair pale face alone
> By the cool bright spring in the hallowed stone; "

her jewelled hand supporting her head, crowned with its
tiara of velvet and pearls, her long brown hair floating
like a veil over her richly-wrought dress, and her slip-
pered feet resting on a smooth slab of Italian marble,
which had been brought there to confine the waters in
the spring.

And thus they found her, sleeping calmly, peacefully,
her eyes closed tightly, and her teeth set firmly together.
There was a strange calmness in Harris' manner, as he
pressed his hand upon her cold, damp brow, and swept
back her long spiral curls. Then, with a quick, excited
glance at her firmly-closed eyes, he gave rapid orders for
a burial-case, such as they always carried with them, to
be brought up, that her body might be placed in it and
carried to Italy. As he raised the inanimate form in his
arms, and laid her head upon a cushion of velvet and

eider-down, a paper floated out from the heavy folds of
her dress, and rested on the stones at his feet. He took
it up; it was a few verses of poetry, traced in the delicate
Italian penmanship of Arabel's own hand. Tears sprang
to the almost girlish eyes of the boy, Carl, as he saw
them.

"She was like a sister to you, was she not, Carl?"
Harris said, kindly, laying his hand upon the boy's head.
A deep sigh was his only answer, and the boy turned
away. Then, drawing a richly-chased knife from a
wrought case by his side, he lifted one of the long ring-
lets from her dress, and turned a beseeching look upon
Harris. "You may have it, Carl," he answered to the
boy's look; and the bright, polished steel glanced in among
the waving hair, until only the gold-tipped haft was
visible.

"What will you do with that, signor?" Carl said,
pointing to the paper. Harris glanced over it, and then
read aloud:

> "Bury me not by the water's edge,
>   Away in my dear old home,
> Nor in the shade of the pure white cliff,
>   Where the screaming sea-gulls come.
> But away, away, on the high hill's brow,
>   Where the dark trees darker wave,
> Ye have found for me a stranger home, —
>   O, give me a stranger grave!"

"I have no one but you to advise me, Carl; now tell
me what to do," Harris said.

Carl looked out at the glowing western sky, and said,
"She will be better pleased if we comply with her last
request; we will bury her here."

Harris only smiled at the boy's reply, and he went on:
"Will you give her to the cold earth decked so showily?
That brilliant, silken, fluttering dress, and those richly-
gleaming pearls, are too earthly for death's bridal, are
they not?"

' "It makes very little difference what the poor, frail
body wears, Carl," Harris answered, mournfully. "We
will bury her as she is."

He did not stop to count the cost of the dress she
wore. There were plenty more of the same kind in the
cases. Then he placed her in the delicately wrought coffin,
only unclasping a single bracelet from her rigid arm, to
be kept as a remembrance of that dark day.

After that the men saw, or imagined, that Harris
grew more stern and changeless in his work, and more
thoughtful in his life, than before. One night, when
they were preparing to leave, he said, "The suspicion
of the colony is aroused; we must keep it up." Then,
taking a slip of paper from his portmanteau, he wrote an
order upon it, and read it aloud. It was for a certain
amount of handcuffs, hatchets, and chains, to be left at
a specified place in the wood, where a quantity of silver,
to their full value, would be found in their stead.

"Which of you will lay this beside the central forge
in the foundery to-night?" he asked, carelessly.

The men drew back, and an involuntary shudder appeared to pass from one to the other. It was the first
time such a subject had been broached. Force had never
been used with them, and they apparently dreaded the
thought of it.

4*

"Stand up, my brave men," said Harris, bitterly; "let me see how many cowards our crew numbers."

Instantly, as though struck by an electric shock, the eight powerful men rose to their feet, and eight strong right hands grasped the sword-hilts by their sides.

Carl's dark blue eyes looked trustfully into his young commander's face, and he said, "Signor, the Madonna looks at you from the bright stars; think you she would not mourn to hear you call the men, that have served you so long and well, cowards?"

"True, Carl; I was angry and unreasonable. Your girlish manliness makes me ashamed of myself," answered Harris; "but I do not like to give up the idea of frightening the colonists. They saw our little sailer last night and yester morn, and will be on the look-out for her again. Here, Roland, I know you are not afraid; take the order, and, to reward you for going, I promise that the manacles shall never be used on you."

Then three cheers for little Carl rung out upon the air, and he lifted the handsome velvet cap from his dark flowing hair, and bowed low to acknowledge the compliment.

Soon after this, Harris returned to Italy, and Don Jose became commander of a clipper of his own, Carl still accompanying him. After Harris had arranged his affairs in Italy, so that they no longer needed his presence, he entirely abandoned the idea of a home on the firm land, and roamed about wherever fancy dictated or news called him. Upon going to their hiding-place in Wales, at one time, he saw a girl, habited in the common dress of Welsh peasants, half sitting, half kneeling, by the road-side, making wreaths and bouquets from a collection of flowers beside her, and placing them in a basket on fresh green leaves.

"Buy flowers, sir? buy flowers?" she asked, as he came up.

"Yes," was the reply, "take all you have; and come with me. I have no way to carry them without your basket, — come."

"Pay, sir?" she said, looking into his face with a roguish, merry smile, making her black eyes dance, and showing her white, even teeth.

Harris laughed, threw a bit of money towards her, and walked on. She gathered up her treasures and followed. They entered the castle, and every man drank to the health of the pretty flower-girl. She drew back trembling, and tried to run away. Harris stopped her, and led her to a low seat where the sunlight looked in, bidding her go on with her work, and when that was finished he had plenty more for her to do. She laughed and pouted, and at last went to work again.

After that she was often at the castle, and at last she too embarked on the waters, to find a home in the new country. There was a dark rumor afloat, at the time, of force used to make the wild Cathrin go with the pirate band; but it was soon forgotten.

After this there were more regular rules observed; only the seven regular members staying at the Glen and the rock, and sometimes only five. Cathrin was given over to Veale, but why it was that she never saw any more of Harris she did not know.

One morning the Arabel shot out of the snug little

harbor of Lynn, with all sail set, the whole crew on
board, and all their hidden treasures left in the sole care
of Cathrin and the magic rattlesnake. But there was
trouble brewing. Even then one of the king's cruisers
was out upon the watch for the little, outlandish craft.
They were well matched as to sailing, but the Britisher's
broadside soon swept away the fore-topmast of the Arabel. Then she was boarded, a hand-to-hand encounter
ensued, and the pirates, instead of being subdued, tri-
umphed, and took the others prisoners. This, of course,
was a flagrant, never-to-be-forgotten offence; but they
kept on their way rejoicing, and at last met Harris at
Wales.

"Where is the little flower-girl?" he asked, as they
sat discussing their business over the flowing wine.

The men looked surprised, and Veale answered, "She
is at the cave, your honor."

"At the cave!" repeated Harris. "Why! was she
willing to go?"

"I don't know — that is — I did n't ask her," answered Veale, stammering at the thought of Harris'
displeasure.

"Well," Harris began, "that is worse than I thought
would be laid at our door just yet. You *mean, low,
detestable, contemptible wretch!*" he added, almost
fiercely, turning to Veale, "do you know what you
have done? actually stolen the only child of fondly-dot-
ing parents, and now trying to excuse yourself. I carried my mistress there, did I? But we were married first
— married by the rites of a church she loved and revered;
besides which, she left neither parents nor friends to

mourn for her, and went because she wished to. I will return with you, Veale," he continued, after a pause, "and bring the birdling back."

It was long before the Arabel again reached America, and when, at dead of the night, the pirates landed and made their way to the Glen, they were unnoticed, for the colonists had grown weary with watching, and given up in despair.

"Will you go home with me, Katy?" Harris said kindly, the next morning, as they reached the rock and commenced partaking of the provisions which the nimble fingers set before them.

Tears came to her dancing black eyes, and she answered, firmly, "I am afraid to go, sir. Can you not bring my mother here?"

Harris smiled, as he asked, "How old are you, Cathrin?"

"Eighteen summers and nineteen winters, sir," she replied, looking at him from under her long lashes.

"Indeed!" said Harris, in surprise; "you look less than that."

A frightened, half-angry look passed her face, as she heard from the furthest end of the cave the heavy voice of Veale swearing at one of the men.

"You are not used to profanity, poor child!" he continued, but she did not reply.

Soon after that another scene came up. Veale had been drinking hard all day, and at night was fairly intoxicated. As Cathrin came into the cave, her head crowned with evergreen, and her hands full of flowers, she heard the merry, musical laugh, which she well knew came

from none but Harris, immediately followed by a volley
of oaths, such as she seldom heard.

"I can drink wine, and not suffer for it in that style,"
he said, "and why cannot you? Come, get up, now, or
by the powers, I will run you through — do you hear?"
and he brandished his glittering sword in true buccanier
style.

Veale was lying upon the floor of the cave, apparently
not too insensible to carry on the joke. Cathrin shrunk
trembling away, and commenced clearing the tea-table.
Her presence did not act as a controlling influence, as
Arabel's had. The men were willing to do anything in
reason for the merry girl, however, and the life she led
at the cave was not altogether intolerable.

Months passed, and a little stranger opened his bright
eyes and claimed protection.

"Who will be thy mother, darling?" Cathrin said,
pleasantly, for she thought she would soon be a spirit.
But things were differently ordered. It was not long
before she was out again, at nightfall, watching for the
arrivals.

And now again pictures darker and more gloomy arise
before our parti-colored glass.

It was early one bright autumn morn that Cathrin
was kneeling by the spring, plashing the cool water over
the flowers she had gathered, to keep them fresh, when
she heard a low, stifled, wailing cry from the beautiful
couch where she had left the child. When she reached
it Veale was walking slowly down the mountain path,
and the babe lay gasping for breath in the sunlight. All
the long day did Cathrin chafe the marble brow and tiny

hands of the insensible child, and at night, when the men returned, she was still holding it in her arms. Harris looked pityingly upon her, and she laid the little form beside him on the silken couch. But the bright-eyed stranger's life had fled. Cathrin was childless.

Again we leave them for a short time, but their crime is not forgotten. They are watched constantly. At last three of them were out at sea, the remaining four were traced to the Glen, and there were taken. Before they reached the vessel that was to convey them to England one escaped. Of course it was the daring Veale, who spurned law and order, and defied pursuit. Harris had been in Italy some time then, and had, therefore, no means of knowing what was going on. Veale fled to the rock, but he was not pursued again. Cathrin lost her merry, life-loving heart, and pined in solitude. Veale used to light signal fires upon rocks to wreck vessels along the coast, and only when she saw him lighting his dark lantern, and preparing his flaming pine knots, could she be won from her silent mournfulness. Then she would talk hours in her thrilling, childish way, and sing to him until her clear voice filled every part of the cavern, and woke the echoes among the gray old rocks; for she dreaded the idea of feeling that her very life was in the keeping of one who would so heedlessly destroy others.

" You will not light the treacherous coys this fearful, stormy eve?" she said, pleadingly. " O, I will sing you all the legends of my Welsh home, and all the songs Roland has taught me, if you will not go now."

Sometimes she would prevail, and he would sit by the

heavy chest that served them for a table, and laugh at
the brilliant fairy tales she wove from her memories of
the dear old home in Wales.

But Cathrin was dying. Day by day her strength
was wasting itself away, her cheek grew paler and thin-
ner, and now a hectic flush burned in lieu of her former
health. Her eyes grew dull and expressionless, and, at
last, she died, her last song just echoing its burden of
victory, and her last glance fixed upon the blue sky and
the gorgeous sunset.

Veale mourned for her as deeply as it was in his power
to mourn for any one, but he dared not bury her; he
lived in constant fear that he, or rather the treasures
there, would be molested; so he raised her in his strong
arms and bore her to the inner room of the cave, then
gently laid her on the shelving rocks, flung the soft folds
of her India muslin over her pale face and staring black
eyes, and went out from the cave alone, a sterner and
more merciless man.

All this time Wallace had been more or less interested
in the pirates and their work. His noble black horse
was often urged over the uneven road by Harris or himself; but now he took himself away, and denied all further
knowledge of the procedure. Veale's provisions were
exhausted. He dared not take the glittering golden
coins to exchange for bread, so he obtained some cheap
work, and determined, for the sake of occupying his mind,
to earn his own food. How long he lived thus, we do
not care to tell, but he gave up his business as wrecker,
now that Wallace refused to assist him, and delivered
him half the profits of their eight months' treachery.

Now we have told the history of Dungeon Rock up to the year one thousand six hundred and fifty-eight, at which time the mortal pilgrimage of Veale was unceremoniously ended by a terrible earthquake, which closed the ancient entrance to the cavern, and thus shut him off from light and life with his dearly-loved treasure, and the superstition-guarded charm and rattlesnake.

From this time forth Dungeon Rock loses its interest; and only a weirdlike fascination hanging round it prevented its being entirely forgotten. It was years before anything more was done there, until, about forty years ago, a man residing in the town adjoining the one where the rock stands became impressed, or, as he styled it, dreamed, that, by going to a certain place in Dungeon Pasture, he could discover treasures formerly buried there by the pirates. He went, as directed, exhumed the treasure, and the probability is, had he been left to follow his own impressions, would have used it to open the rock.

As it was, his nearest relatives took the matter up, hushed the stories that were getting afloat about the money, accused the man of insanity, and took the *trash* into their own hands. This seemed to have an undue effect upon the mind of the man, whose name was Brown. He had always been singularly nervous and impressible. When young he could commit a lesson almost at a glance, and recite it with perfect accuracy. As he grew older, he became morbid and sensitive; would sit for hours talking or singing, his face lighted up with a strange smile, which, when he was aroused from his half trance, would pass away, and he become cross and peevish as before.

After finding the money in Dungeon Pasture, he dwelt more upon such things than before, and often expressed a determination to run away, — a threat which he afterward put into execution, finding there was no way for him to recover his rightful property. He wandered away down east, where he spent several years, and occasionally told his strange story. It was by that that he was again discovered and brought back to his home, where, by bribes and threats, he was induced to leave off telling the story. He never could be induced to work; for he constantly averred that he had enough to make him independent, and, if they would let him alone, he knew where he could find plenty more. He has always been supported, however, by those who were said to have the management of what he found; and, upon the death of his last near relative, a half-brother, he was placed in the Ipswich asylum for incurable insane people, where he will probably remain until his death.

The next movement of consequence was years afterward, when the city of Lynn was said to have footed the bills for any quantity of ammunition, to be used for the purpose of making a grand attack upon the obstinate rock, and forcing it to give up its trust. It proved a failure, and the city never paid the bills, either; but, many a quiet night after that, sober, respectable men laughed at each other about their fast-day blow. Their object was to fill all the principal crevices with powder, and have them explode in such a manner as would shatter the rock into a countless number of pieces, and thus lay open the inside of it, and the cave, if there were any there.

Some went away satisfied that all had been done that could be, and there was no treasure there; others, that the original cave and its contents remained undisturbed; but all agreed that they had ventured their share upon the sea of speculation, and should not try again right away.

Soon after this, mesmeric clairvoyance became one of the reigning topics of the day, and almost immediately the interest of Dungeon Rock was again agitated.   This time, one of the world-renowned singing brothers, Jesse Hutchinson, was the chief actor, directed by a mesmerized lady, who steadily affirmed the truth of the disconnected history that had been handed down to them, and added her declarations to those who had firmest faith in the old saying of wealth in Dungeon Cave.

The operations flagged not for days and weeks; and, when at last Jesse gave it up, not as a delusion, but as a task too hard for him, others kept on, and made the hole still deeper and broader.   But they too failed, and, for a long time, the hill was undisturbed save by occasional picnic parties, or Sunday groups of young people, who went there to enjoy themselves.

Now our scene changes from the quiet, unfrequented, hilly woodland, to the limitless plains of the great West, where the waters of America's broadest and deepest lake ceaselessly lave its shores.   It is the hour of a boat landing, and any number of men, women, and children, could be seen hurrying to the wharf, with the first whole dish they could reach, be it wash-bowl, ewer, or skillet, teapot, pan, or pail; and one general cry of "whiskey, whiskey," was heard throughout the ranks.

In a small building, that served for kitchen, parlor, and bedroom, to quadruped and biped, two men, apparently near the same age, and both past the years of youth, sat, or rather reclined, talking busily with each other.

"Rum is a great curse, Marble."

"Granted."

"And, if a great deal ruins a man, a little, be it ever so little, injures him."

"Granted also, Long; but now look here. In our crew there are only men; but I warrant that up yonder, when the boat landed, you might have seen people of all kinds and colors flocking to the wharf. You well know what they were after. Now, answer me this one question. Would it not be better for us to set the example by keeping whiskey for our own gang, and thus prevent their going to the boat, than it is to apparently countenance beastly drunkenness, by their drinking all they can obtain at irregular intervals?"

Long hesitated, and Marble went on.

"I know your principles. I know you consider rum-drinking as the one unpardonable sin; but, if you stop to think about it, you may bring your orthodoxy to agree with my infidelity.

"It may be so," Long added, after a pause. "I have thought a great deal on this subject, and am not yet decided. You have sold rum, have you not?"

Marble nodded.

"Well, do you think what you have sold has done most — which? — good, or bad?"

"Bad," was the prompt reply.

"I thought as much," answered Long; "but that is not what I was going to speak of just now. I want to know how you would like the idea of keeping a boarding-house."

"First-rate," answered Marble. "We could drive four stakes into the ground, stretch a bit of cloth over them, and name it the Marquet Eating Saloon, where shall be kept all manner of provisions, viz., whiskey, to be had at the shortest notice." And a droll smile rested in the corners of Marble's mouth, and twinkled in his small eyes, as he ceased speaking; while Long, as the picture came vividly before his active imagination, threw his head back and laughed loud and long.

"That is not what I wanted, Hiram," he said, soon stopping his mirth and growing sober again. "There are a great plenty of such establishments going up in all parts of the country. We need a real framed house; and, if you would plan such a one as you think you could keep properly, why, all is, we would find means to build it, and have it done right away. You shall bring your wife on to manage, and your children to inhabit it. You shall keep on being overseer. I will be a wealthy land-holder. Jointly and severally we shall be honored for inventing, or, rather, for starting the great Marquet Iron Works, and, by my faith, we shall live fat."

Then the two men separated, each to his own place; and here it may not be inapropos to describe them.

Long, who appeared to be chief director there, was tall, but rather slightly built, with a long face, intelligent-looking, dark eyes, a high, but not full brow, and thin lips, that partially disclosed a regular set of teeth.

Marble, who seemed like Long's very right hand, was also tall, but strong and robust, with sharp, bright blue eyes, light waving brown hair, and a full white brow.

On the night after their conversation, which we have recorded, Marble, who always, as Long said, if he put his hands to the plough, not only did not look back, but did not look forward either, and only attended to holding the plough, started from the settlement to reach a small hill at a little distance, partly to select trees from the lot for their house, and partly to think over the practicability of the scheme they had been discussing. He was walking slowly along, with his eyes fixed upon the ground, when, suddenly looking up, he found himself back to the place whence he started.

"Can't you go as far as you can see?" he muttered to himself, starting again for the wood; but again he became lost in thought, and again he found himself at the same place.

"Well, if you can't go as far as you can see, you may go home," he said, casting a regretful look at the woodland, and turning away. It was a habit he always had of talking to himself, and it saved him many hours of trouble.

Soon after this, he started for his home away in old Massachusetts, which, upon reaching, he found was not entirely exempt from the joint hands of time and sorrow. He had been at home from the West but a short time, when his youngest child, a boy of thirteen, was taken sick; and thus his plans were frustrated. His sickness was short and painful; and his burning cheeks and glassy bright eyes told but too plainly to the father's heart that George's days were numbered.

About this time he, too, became interested in clairvoyance. Before going West, he had, at the request of a friend, consulted a phrenological subject, who predicted his departure, and also his misfortune — for such she termed the death in the family. After finishing her talk, she informed him that she sometimes told fortunes; and asked if she might tell his.

He did not care about it; had little faith in such things, etc.; but, if she would like to, he had no objections.

She run the cards over, and told him essentially what she had said before; adding that, in the course of a specified time, she thought he would be in steady business.

He was, at the time, all ready to go West with a party of men to establish the Marquet Iron Works.

He went and returned. George died; but, as yet, no steady employment presented itself.

While staying in Marquet, a young man, an entire stranger in Massachusetts, had described Dungeon Rock to him as his place to work, but told no names, even of the town or state where it lay. He was, at that time, careless, or even sceptical about the matter; but, after George's death, he aroused himself, and concluded to investigate, and, if he could, to understand the subject.

He came to Lynn, and, subsequently, to a distant relative in a neighboring town. Here he staid some time; and, upon one occasion, feeling unwell, he determined to consult a clairvoyant in the place, who was entirely unacquainted with him or his business. Accordingly, he expressed a desire to have him consulted, and Mr. Wheeler, who was going to a neighboring town, offered to stop and see him, and, perhaps, invite him to his house, as Mr. Marble was there staying.

He went, and, as he entered the room and made known his errand, the clairvoyant, whose name was Emerson, commenced talking, and finally seated himself at the table, and began to write with great rapidity, speaking now and then to ask or answer questions, and taking very little notice of his work.

He was young, apparently less than twenty years of age; but his dark complexion and keen black eyes gave a look of maturity, which his slight, almost petite figure, and long curling hair, instantly contradicted. When he stopped writing, he folded and directed the letter, and gave it to Mr. W. without a word of comment, having first signed his own name to it as a medium.

"But the gentleman thought he might want to see you on some other business," Wheeler said, doubtfully, holding the document between his thumb and finger.

"I presume it is there, sir," was the reply; and the medium turned away.

Mr. Wheeler left the house, and, instead of keeping on his way, concluded to return with the letter. He did so; and, entering the room where Mr. Marble was, gave him the letter, and told him to read it aloud.

Marble did so; and, before he reached the end, Wheeler threw his hat upon the floor, and asked what he would take for half the rock, as he, Wheeler, would like to go into company with him.

Marble did not answer until he had devoured the whole contents of the letter, which really contained a great many mysterious and some unaccountable statements concerning the business in which he then was engaged. Among others, it stated that he would call there the next day and go with them to the rock; which he did, accompanied by a friend who generally mesmerised or put him to sleep. He threw himself upon the ground beside the rock, when he reached it, and, after becoming entranced, told how and where they must work, etc.

And, now that we have got them fairly started, we will go back a single year, and try if we can tell a reasonable story. Soon after George's death, as we have said before, Mr. M. aroused himself, and determined to investigate the subject of mesmerism. Opportunities soon presented themselves. When staying at a public house, one night, the porter came to him and said, "Madame Y. is here, and wishes to see you."

"Who is Madame Y.?" he asked, thoughtfully.

"I don't know," was the reply; "but she sent her name, and bade me say she had told your fortune."

An indistinct recollection seemed to cross his mind, but he only said, "I will go," and was accordingly conducted into her presence.

She recalled their former meeting, inquired as to the veracity of what she had then said, and ended by telling him there was a very good clairvoyant, Madame Maine, with her at that time, and, if he liked, she would put her to sleep and have him examined.

He was at the time suffering from a recent attack of the Asiatic cholera, which was accurately described by

Madame M., even to the time and place of his sickness,
for which she wrote a prescription, which he took in all
faith.

She then went on to tell what he was to do for the
future. "You will dig for a pirate's money," she said,
"and will find" — here she hesitated.

"A bugbear," he said, laughing.

"The pirate, himself, sir," she added, "or, rather,
what there is left of what was once a pirate, and a treasure with him."

"That is encouraging," he said, concealing his unbe-
lief. "Can you tell me where this money lies that I am
to dig for?"

"It is somewhere by the sea-side, I think," she answered; "less than twenty miles from Boston."

Well, he left with his confidence in mesmerism so much
lessened that he never used his prescription. A short
time after that he met two or three young men convers-
ing upon that subject. They had heard something of
Mr. M.'s experience, and wanted to hear more.

"What is the most likely thing they ever told you?"
one asked.

"That I should go to digging for money," he replied.

A burst of laughter followed this grave assertion, and
they asked to have it explained.

"Well, the truth is this. Madame Maine told me that
I was soon to be engaged in searching, or rather digging,
for a pirate and his money."

"Do you know where it is?" asked one, whose name
was Olds.

Marble laughed at the thoughtful look which had

settled on their faces, and answered, "No; she gave out when she had got about so far, and could not tell the rest."

"I'll warrant it was down in Lynn!" exclaimed Olds.

"What do you know about Lynn?" Marble asked.

"I have been there, myself," he answered, earnestly; "and I have no doubt that there is money there. At any rate, I advise you to go and try it."

Soon after this Marble consulted a physician, who told him that he needed a change; the salt air would be good for him; he had better pay the sea-shore a visit. This decided him, for, as he afterwards expressed it, everybody and everything he met seemed to be pointing him away, away.

"I will go and work a fortnight," he said; and nobly well has his word been kept.

Upon this he went and took a survey of the rock. It contained a huge chasm, which he thought would lead to a cave, *if there was one*, with a very little trouble. He commenced work in company with two other men, and made slow work of it, too, as the rock was very hard, and they had nothing to direct their motions, and nothing but hope to live upon as far as the work in the rock was concerned.

It was about a year that they worked thus; then first one man, and soon the other, became weary and discouraged, and left. The cave was still as far distant as ever; faith had grown weak, and hope, which formed so tempting a breakfast, seemed about to prepare a very poor supper.

It is about this time that we find how great is the power of perseverance. Mr. Marble, after the other men had left, continued the work for some time with his only son, a young man about twenty years of age. And thus it was, after working a year by the guidance of mesmerism, that we find him consulting the first *clairvoyant medium*, and this led him into the mystic labyrinths of spiritualism, or spiritual philosophy.

The grounds which the medium took were substantially these: that when, by the action of his friend's mind, he was rendered unconscious, some disembodied spirit took possession of him, and told what living people did or did not know. He told Mr. Marble how to work in the hole he had excavated, and, at one time, foretold a circumstance which was of considerable importance. It was that within a certain number of hours he would find a something to encourage him. It did not tell what, and the number of hours included a week's time. Four days after that, an ancient-looking, rusty sword, with a leather-wound haft and a brass-bound scabbard, was found in a large seam inside the rock. Soon after being exposed to the air, the leather upon the handle crumbled away, and the thick, blue mould on the brass began to wear off. The chasm in the rock is still shown to visitors, and the prints where the sword lay in the clayey soil were once to be seen, but have since been removed, in the hopes of finding more relics.

This was a great event to build a hope upon, and it had its full effect on the spirits of those interested. Dungeon Rock soon became a place of particular interest to mediums. The well-known Mrs. Pike paid it a visit; also

Mrs. Freeman, who had, on a former occasion, directed Mr. Marble to go to a certain street and number, in the city of Boston, where he would find an aged, bed-ridden woman, who would be of use to him.

He went, and discovered Madame Lamphier, to whom he made known his errand as one who had come to have his fortune told.

"Fortin'! who says I tell fortins'?" was the spiteful ejaculation that greeted him.

"Well, what do you tell?" he asked, convinced that she was the one he sought.

"Why, I have a stone that I look in, and if any one has business, it generally comes up here," she replied, doggedly.

"Well, I should like to have you look into it for me," he said, in a conciliatory manner.

Accordingly she drew out her stone, adjusted her glasses, and commenced by seeing him in a deep, dark hole, with something hung up between himself and a pile of gold which he was trying to reach. She then kept on, and described a young girl, as she saw her, about twelve years of age, who was to be of future service to him or his work. "And you will not get through with the partner you have now, either!" she said, decidedly.

"Well, I was told that same thing about my last partner," he muttered, half to himself and half aloud.

"What was his name?" she asked.

"What do you think?" he answered, Yankee fashion.

"I see a large W.," she said, musingly.

"Well, that is right; his name was Wheeler," he replied. "What do you think of him?"

6

"I don't know nothing about him," said the old woman, cautiously; "but I see one very mean thing that
he did."

"You mean to say he is a dishonest man, then?" Mr.
Marble said, for the sake of getting along faster.

"No, I don't," she said, fearfully; "he is not dishonest, but he took the advantage."

"Well, never mind that, tell me about my present
partner; do you know *his* name?" Marble said again,
to turn the theme.

"I see the same large W.," she said, "but it looks
finer and handsomer.

"Really, quite a compliment; anything more?"

"Yes; I see a great deal of wood."

"Well, it is the land that I work on, — is it not?"

"No; it is something in connection with your partner. I see him now. He is young — light-complected
for a black-eyed person. There is something strange
about his eyes; they glare at me like coals of fire. He
is not very handsome, but there is a taking way with him
that makes the gentlefolks like him at first sight. Splen-
did young fellow, ah!"

"Yes," said Marble, "fine man; is he not?"

An Indian-like grunt escaped her, and she said, "You
have not told me what that wood means."

"Wood — why, it is his name — is it not?"

"Yes, — I think so. It is gone now," she said, and
prepared to lay aside her stone.

"You spoke about his being young; is he not old
enough for that work?" Marble asked.

"In years he is," she answered, moodily.

"Not old enough in business, then, you meant," he continued.

"In iniquity, did you say?" she asked.

Mr. M. saw he could get nothing more from her that day, and soon took his leave.

Time passed. Mr. Marble's confidence was betrayed, and his plans frustrated. Mr. Wood took the whole responsibility upon himself, and tried to buy the rock. Finding he was foiled in this, he hired a man to go to work against Mr. Marble. In this he failed also, and, instead of getting the other half of the business, he lost the half he already had. After this Mr. Marble had no more partners. The man Mr. Wood had hired kept on working there in his own employ. Marble had built a small house for his own accommodation some time before, and one or another of his or Mr. Wheeler's family had done the work there, and kept them comfortable. Now the hired man offered to bring his wife there to reside, which he did a short time before Mr. Wood left. Mr. Marble's family had been staying in the vicinity a while, but long before cold weather they returned to their home in the interior, and nothing now remained to cheer the unbroken monotony of his way. The long and chilling winter of the year eighteen hundred and fifty-five will be remembered a great while by the man whose work was to find a way into Dungeon Rock.

With the summer came plenty and warmth again; the little garden was planted, the carriage road laid out and built, where before there was scarcely a path; a friend gave him two hundred dollars, to be refunded when he found himself able. With this he laid the foundation for a large stone building, to be erected in the octagon form, somewhat after the fashion of the gray and sombre Oriad. Then another person, seemingly still more of a friend, was directed (also by the spirits) to forward two or three thousand dollars to have the work go on. This was a brilliant proposal; but, owing to some mismanagement or mistake, it was never carried into effect.- A short time before this a spring was discovered upon the low land near the rock, which proved to be a great curiosity. Then a small wooden house was erected, in addition to the one already there, into which the remainder of Mr. Marble's family, consisting of a wife and daughter, removed.

Soon after this, a party of people from Charlestown and Boston, who had lately become interested in the place, were there on a visit, when a medium, being entranced, purported to speak from the spirit of Sir Walter Scott, and requested a lady who was present to make Mr. M. a present, such as he (the spirit) would dictate. It afterwards came in the shape of a flag-staff, eighty feet in length, which was firmly planted in the place formerly excavated by the Hutchinsons. Then a flag with the appropriate inscription, "Thy faith is founded on a rock," was raised upon it by the lady's own hands. There was no fear of starvation that winter, but the snow was wondrously deep, and the hollows were piled softly up, almost even with the hill-tops.

When the spring opened, company came thronging again to the rock, to see and hear all that was wonderful and strange; for the popularity of the place had been steadily increasing, and the world is ever on the look-out for something new. All that spring and summer company and visitors, picnic parties and relatives, were coming in rapid succession, and no material change was made, either in the work or their way of life.

Fresh, dreamy September, like a maiden just passing from childhood to her teens, came softly on. There is but one more incident of interest to note; *that* is, when the great philanthropist, and remarkable medium, John M. Spear, paid it a passing visit, in company with two or three other mediums.

And now our history is finished.

There is a small room, away up in the very top of a block of buildings, where the sun beats scorchingly down, and the dust whirls in clouds through the narrow street. And there, where affluence is unknown, and elegance unconsulted, — where no rich tapestry shields the artist's easel from the light, — is a work of magic art and mystic mystery, which has been seen by hundreds, and will be by thousands. It is a rare, bright picture — a childish, dimpled face, with deep, wondrous blue eyes, and thick clustering curls; one round arm is flung over the shaggy neck of a large black dog, as if to show how perfectly the spiritual part of nature can overcome the animal; and the whole picture represents some half-embodied ideal, which is in future years to become a reality. There are, undoubtedly, the touches of the old artists, Ben West, Raphael, and Angelo, about the work, and their power may not be yet extinct; but the world is not ready for such ideas as yet; it must receive the truth gradually.

But, the picture of " Natty, a spirit," has nothing to

do with our present work. It is its executor of whom
we would speak. He is an artist of some celebrity, and
his painting of the spirit child has made him famous.
He professes to have distinct visions of spirits in human
form; snatches of landscapes, birds, flowers, and, indeed,
almost everything that can be seen in the natural
world. He is a reflective, and rather a peculiar man;
there are silvery threads in his hair, and furrows on his
brow, as though he thought a great deal. And he it is
that has been chosen to do the work of planning and
directing the laying out of Dungeon Pasture, which is to
be called "Iowah;" a name which the red man gave it
long ago, and which signifies "I have found it."

The legend of that name is as follows: "Several
hundred years ago the united forces of pestilence, famine,
and war, had so reduced a large tribe of Indians, that
only a very few remained, and, after calling a council of
their wisest men, these few determined to leave the home
of their fathers and found a new settlement; accordingly,
they started through the trackless wild on their vague
expedition; they passed

> "Through tangled juniper, beds of reeds,
> Through many a fen where the serpent feeds,
> And man never trod before;"

and at last came to the foot of a large hill, with an
enormous ledge upon the top. Upon climbing this, they
saw spread out before them a panoramic view of what
they knew would prove a good hunting-ground, for it
had forests for game and water for fish. Then a loud
cry of "Iowah! Iowah!" made the welkin ring, and the

whole party encamped that night in the large, open cave,
before commencing their work. They called the river
Sauguas, which means broad or extended, and when the
tribe grew large and strong, and reached away down to
the great "Father of Waters," they called the two
beaches Nahaunte, which means the brothers, or the
twins.

All this is to be revived again ; the woodland to be laid
out in groves, and parks, and forests ; the spring in the
cave to be cleared again, and its brink bordered by
marble slabs ; the ancient, scattered treasures will be
gathered-up, bright, flashing diamonds, clear white seed-
pearls, with heavy gold settings, and antique jewelry and
ornaments, that have been a long time lying useless.
The heavy, iron-bound box, that was left there, has been
disturbed and broken by the action of the earth, and its
contents are now duly mixed up with equal quantities of
dirt, loose stones, and rubbish, which the water from the
spring, all choked up as it is, has for the space of two
hundred consecutive years been laving. There was once
a case of silks left there, but, as the cave is not perfectly
air and water tight, the probability is that, although they
look the same as ever, there is not much durability to
them. The grave of Arabel, Veale levelled down, but
the spot is still pointed out by mediums, and, although
the tree under which Harris laid her has long since
decayed, another has grown up very near where that was
supposed to stand, which is now in the centre of a thriv-
ing garden.

Cathrin's sepulchre is the "rock of ages," and traces

of her remains will be found upon one of the shelving places within the cave. The child was buried, but

> " The string of pearls and the lock of hair,
> And the ring of gold that it used to wear,"

will be found by Cathrin's side, where Veale, with his superstitious reverence, placed them.

The cave will be found in two separate apartments, beside the entrance, which clairvoyant mediums see as another room. Veale, himself, or rather his bones, will be found in the outer, or largest room, together with the remains of his shoe-making tools. The other contents of the rock we leave for time to discover, and the sagacity of the " Excavator " to make known.

The medium that Madame Lamphier saw four years ago, at the age of twelve, has been employed more or less, for five or six weeks past, in writing this little work, which we now send on its way, without a single fear that its mission will be ever unaccomplished. The time for all things to be done is ordered; and when we have said all that can be known about such a place as Dungeon Rock, there still remains one question unanswered — one doubt unremoved. Time alone can verify what hundreds have told, either by impression, clairvoyance, or entrancement, that there still remains a cave there, and that the present laborer, Mr. Hiram Marble, otherwise known as the Excavator, shall be the one to discover it.

LINES COMMUNICATED TO A CIRCLE AT DUNGEON ROCK,
FEBRUARY 22D, 1856.

FAR away from the voice of the rolling sea
A noble banner is waving free,
With its motto of blue on a pure white ground,
And a single stripe of scarlet around.
America's tri-color, red, white, and blue,
Flutters softly there all the long day through.
On the high, firm rock, 'bove the grassy strand,
With its heavy brace, does the flag-staff stand;
While not far down on the rough hill's side
Is the small, rude cot, where the workers abide.
We know, ere the cold winter flitted o'er,
That want peered in through the opened door;
But hearts were willing to boldly strive,
And hope and faith kept the soul alive;
So, spite of famine's half-looked-for shock,
The work still prospered in Dungeon Rock.
Strong hands kept picking the stone chips out,
And forcing the long, circuitous route;
Strong hearts were waiting, for well they knew
That summer would bring them enough to do.
With curious eyes, and a curious name,
Or open purses and open fame.
But the stranger's scorn and the stranger's love
Were never valued true friends above.

Years pass like the hours of a summer day,
And leave no memento to mark their stay.

We have told of the faith in the Rock alive
In the year eighteen hundred and fifty-five;
Let us turn Time's current, and backward go,
And see what new wonders her book will show,
By skipping two centuries, just to derive
The knowledge of sixteen fifty-five.

There's a still, dark wood, and a winding stream,
Where the cold, bright stars, and the moon's pale beam,
Light up a low path, by the underbrush hid,
And gild the smooth plate on the coffer's dull lid.
There are hurrying footsteps and stifled tones
In that lonely ravine of earth and stones;
'T is the hiding-place of a pirate band,
Who came from a distant, brilliant land,
And their burden of spoils from the broad, high seas
They have borne to that forest of woodland trees,
Where the wild wolf howls in his dismal den,
Or makes his home in that pirate's glen.
They are startled now, those men so brave,
And are taking their treasure to Dungeon Cave.
Away through the wood that once skirted the vale
They had made for themselves an invisible trail;
And, now that the night was so dark and still,
They were moving their spoils from the glen to the hill.
An iron-bound box, with its shining gold,
And a limestone fossil, pure and cold,
On its soft, white cotton, was resting there,
Treasured with superstitious care.
There are noble hearts in that lonely home,
And Harris, the leader, is soon to come.
They hear him now, as they firmly tread
O'er the fallen leaves and the flowers dead:

"Halt!" — the low, deep summons is soon obeyed,
And Harris moves out from the tall tree's shade.
There's a light in his eye, and a stern command
In the haughty wave of his ungloved hand,
As he lifts the cap from his high, white brow,
And says, "My men, be ready now.
Have you ta'en the strong box from the vessel's hold,
And well secured it, with all its gold?
Have you counted the diamonds we stole from the berth
Of the fair Cristelle, on that night of mirth?
Have you closed my coffers? In short, my men,
Have you cleared all the trash from our silent glen?
For I have an inkling, from what I have heard,
By the foundery, to-night, that the settlers have stirred,
And will soon be for finding the men of ease,
That dare to murder on God's high seas."
"We have moved them all," was the men's reply,
As Harris gazed at the moonlit sky;
"We have moved them all; but what, your honor,
Shall we do, to-night, with our fair Madonna?
Shall we leave her alone in the glen to abide?
Will she make for Sir Wolf a fitting bride?
Or, will she tell tales when they come to look?
For I'll risk a woman to find our nook."
"Peace!" thundered Harris, "and no more fun;
Ye are seven in number, in purpose one."
He added, more kindly, "But now, move on,
For to-night our labor must all be done."
Then he quickly turned toward the lonely glen,
And left in the darkness that band of men.
We can tell no more. But the lady fair,
Ere the next day's sunshine reached her there,
Had followed the winding, woody road,

And found on the hill-side a new abode.
At noon she saw, from the high cave door,
A party of men and torches four
Creep slowly in through the tangled green,
Where the pirate robbers had last been seen.
Three times did the lady fair look down;
Three sunsets she saw on that little town;
Then she rested her fair, pale face alone,
By the cool, bright spring, in the hollowed stone;
And that night, when the pirates came home from the dell,
They buried the form of proud Arabel.
Then years passed on, and another bride
Blessed the cavern home on the high hill-side;
But the pirates were traced to their home by the sea,
And, of all the seven, there escaped but three.
One of these fled to his rocky home,
And dared not away from the cave to roam.
But the merry Cathrin, the pirate's bride,
Mourned out her young life, that year, and died.
And the sturdy Veale, who could ever bear
The darkest storm of both sea and air,
Became a coward, and dared not brave
The suspicious look of a lowly grave.
So he carefully laid that form of clay
On a shelving rock in the cave away;
And he flung the pure folds of her own white dress
O'er her marble brow, in that dark recess.
Then he wandered on, and lived, and grew,
Like the rest of Lynn people, tied to a shoe;
For he dared not betray the gold, so bright,
Lest he should be murdered, some silent night.
But, at last, the great earth felt the earthquake's shock,
And Veale was immured in the prison rock.

Then time fled on, and the silent life
Of nature alone by the rock was rife;
Till the baby city had a regular blow,
Which shattered the stones to their base so low,
And rattled them down till they closed the mouth
Which the earthquake had left toward the sunny south.
The good effects which this blowing made
Were to use the powder, and help the trade.
Then again was the solitude deep and still,
By the pirate glen, and on Dungeon Hill.
But curious minds spied the legends out,
And a new scene of labor was brought about.
A mesmeric lady, of wondrous fame,
And a band of brothers, with as wide a name,
Became interested, and tried for a while
The rocks of the Dungeon's high roof to unpile.
But, though they grew faint, we believing ones say
That Jesse the talented, Jesse the gay,
The brother that shone, ere he passed from sight,
Like a trammelled star of unbounded might,
This scene of his labor has not forgot,
But is lingering still round the lonely spot,
Where the brothers shall some time again unite,
And sing for the dungeon with all their might.
The good they did is, that the heavy bole
Of the flag-staff rests low in the Hutchinson hole.
Then, again, the excitement of Dungeon Rock
Forgot to be the general every-day talk;
And the forest was valued, like other land,
For the visible worth on its rocky strand.
For long, long years was the silence unbroke,
Save the owlet's dull hoot, or the woodpecker's stroke.
But, lo! the hill-side must once and again

Be made to resound to the works of men;
And a long, dark cavern tells half the fears
And all the hopes of long, weary years.

Now, onward we go, for a century more,
To tell of the change that has flitted o'er.
There are lofty mansions, and spacious domes,
And silvery fountains, and pleasant homes;
There are green, bright trees, and flowers gay,
Where now the dark forests so gloomily sway;
And, most of all, is an open cave,
And a clear, pure spring the gray rocks lave;
And the plate-glass protects, without hiding a room,
Where the relics of age and piratical gloom
Are treasured in safety, not for their worth,
But because they had rested so long in the earth;
And the brilliant oxygen light at night
Half shames the moon, with its pure, pale light;
While a painted balloon, with its rubber case,
Floats gracefully down to its proper place,
As though it were waiting the moment when
It could fly far away 'bove the homes of men,
And be guided with equal precision and ease
As far or as near as the rider may please.
And the flag-staff glows with its highland plaid,
With which the painter the bare stick clad;
While high 'bove the earth, in his own free pride,
Is old Red Jacket standing, his bow beside,
And carelessly pointing to those below
The way the wild winds in the cloud regions blow;
And the gay, pure flag, with its tri-colors bright,
Is floating now to the morning light;
But around the bright scarlet, that once was its edge,

Is a border of flowers, 'bove the rocky ledge ;
'T is England's emblem, the roses bright,
And Scotia's thistle, pale, green, and white ;
The shamrock, that Erin's children love,
And the iris and fuschia that droop above.
All these shall be gathered together there,
While the workers faint not on the hillside bare ;
And, at last, when the triumph is made complete,
Shall be woven together these flowers sweet ;
And hundreds and thousands yet shall see
The flower-bordered banner waving free.

And now I have finished this history true
Of the present, the past, and the future, too ;
And all ye great world, whether timid or brave,
Look out for the next news from Dungeon Cave!

ENESEE.